W9-COA-125

Rapunzel
Story Jacob & Wilhelm Grimm
Illustrations Maja Dusíková

The Frog Prince
Story Jacob & Wilhelm Grimm
Illustrations Binette Schroeder

The Snow Queen
Story Hans Christian Andersen
Illustrations Bernadette Watts

Cinderella
Story Charles Perrault
Illustrations Loek Koopmans

The Princess & the Pea
Story Hans Christian Andersen
Illustrations Dorothée Duntze

© 2007 by North-South Books Inc., an imprint of NordSüd Verlag AG, Zürich, Switzerland.
This 2007 edition published by Backpack Books
by arrangement with North-South Books Inc., New York.

All rights reserved. No part of this publication may be reproduced,
stored in a retrieval system, or transmitted, in any form or by any means,
electronic, mechanical, photocopying, recording, or otherwise,
without prior written permission from the publisher.

ISBN-13: 978-0-7607-9369-5
ISBN-10: 0-7607-9369-7

Printed and bound in China

1 3 5 7 9 10 8 6 4 2

Princess Fairy Tales

BACKPACKBOOKS
○
NEW YORK

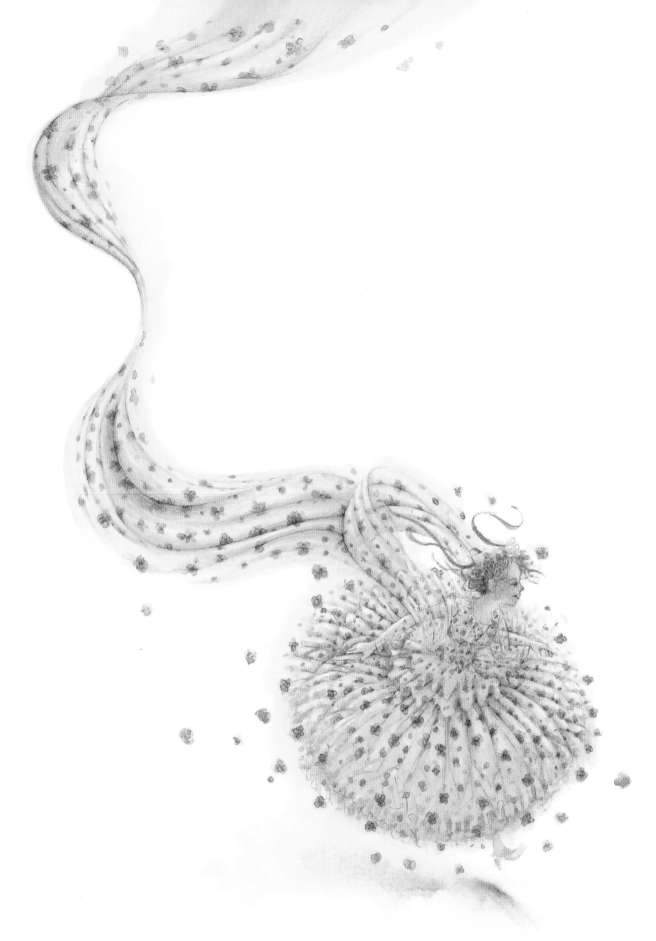

Table of Contents

8

RAPUNZEL

ONCE UPON A TIME there were a man and a woman who had wanted a child for a very long time, but in vain. At last, however, the woman believed the good Lord was going to grant her wish.

From her house she could see a lovely garden full of the most beautiful flowers and delicious herbs, but no one ever dared go into that garden, because it belonged to a powerful witch.

One day the woman stood at her window looking down into the garden, and saw a bed where the salad herb called rampion, or rapunzel, grew. The woman felt a great longing to eat some of those herbs. She wanted them more and more every day, and since she could not get any rapunzel from the garden, she became weak, pale, and miserable. Her husband was alarmed.

"What is the matter, dear wife?" he asked.

"Oh," she said, "I'll die if I can't have some of that rapunzel to eat!"

Her husband, who loved her dearly, said to himself: I can't let my wife die! I must get her some of those herbs, at any price!

When twilight fell that evening, he climbed over the wall into the witch's garden, hastily picked a handful of rapunzel, and brought it home to his wife.

She made it into a salad at once, and ate it greedily. But, she enjoyed the rapunzel so much that the next day she wanted it three times as much as before! She asked her husband to climb over the wall into the witch's garden again.

So when twilight fell, he climbed over the wall once more, but when he was down in the garden he had a dreadful scare, for he saw the witch herself there in front of him.

"How dare you climb into my garden like a thief and steal my rapunzel!" she said angrily. "You'll be sorry for this!"

"Oh, please, have mercy!" begged the man. "I did it only out of desperation. My wife saw your rapunzel from the window, and longed for it so much that she said she would die if she didn't have some to eat!"

At that the witch relented slightly and said, "Very well, you can have as much of my rapunzel as you like, but on one condition. You must give me the baby your wife is about to bear. It will be well looked after. I will care for it like a mother."

In his fear, the man agreed to everything, and as soon as his wife had her baby, the witch appeared, named the little girl Rapunzel, and carried her off.

Rapunzel grew into the loveliest child under the sun. When she was twelve years old, however, the witch shut her up in a tower that stood in the middle of the forest and had neither stairs nor a door. When the witch wanted to get in, she would stand at the foot of the tower and call: "*Rapunzel, Rapunzel, let down your hair!*"

Rapunzel had beautiful long hair, as fine as spun gold, and as soon as she heard the witch's voice, she would take her long braid and wind it around a hook by the window. Then her hair fell down and down, all the way to the ground, and the witch used it to climb up.

One day, the king's son happened to be riding through the forest, and as he passed the tower, he heard such a beautiful song that he stopped to listen. It was Rapunzel, singing sweetly to pass the time in her lonely tower.

The prince wanted to climb up to her, and looked for a doorway into the tower, but there was no door to be found.

He rode home, but the song had moved his heart so much that he went back to the forest every day to hear it.

One day, when the prince was standing behind a tree, he saw the witch come along and heard her call: "*Rapunzel, Rapunzel, let down your hair!*" Then Rapunzel let her braid of hair down, and the witch climbed up to her.

If that's the way up into the tower, thought the prince, then I'll try it myself.

The next day, when dusk was falling, the prince went to the tower and called: "*Rapunzel, Rapunzel, let down you hair!*" Rapunzel let her hair down at once, and the king's son climbed up.

At first Rapunzel was alarmed to see the king's son come in, for she had never set eyes on a man before. However, the prince began talking to her gently, and told her that his heart had been so moved by her singing that he could not rest until he saw her for himself.

Then Rapunzel forgot her fears, and when he asked if she would marry him, she said yes, and put her hand in his.

"I will go with you gladly," she said, "but it will be difficult for me to get down from this tower. Every time you come to see me, you must bring me a silken cord. I'll weave a ladder out of the cords, and when it's ready I will climb down, and you can carry me off on your horse."

They agreed that the prince would visit her every evening until the ladder was ready, for the old witch only came in the daytime.

The witch noticed nothing until one day, without thinking, Rapunzel asked her, "Tell me, Godmother, how is it that you seem so much heavier than the young prince when you climb up?"

"Oh, you wicked child!" cried the witch. "What's all this? I thought I'd shut you safely away from the whole world, but you've tricked me!"

In her fury, she seized Rapunzel's lovely hair and snip, snap, cut it all off! There lay the beautiful braid on the floor. The witch had no pity on poor Rapunzel, and took her to live alone in a deserted part of the forest.

That very evening, the witch fastened the braid of hair she had cut off to the hook by the window, and when the king's son came and called: "*Rapunzel, Rapunzel, let down your hair,*" she let the hair down.

The king's son climbed up. At the top of the tower, however, he found not his beloved Rapunzel, but the witch, glaring at him with venomous rage.

"Aha," she said scornfully, "so you've come for your sweetheart, have you? Well, the pretty bird has flown and won't be singing anymore. The cat has caught her, and will soon scratch out your own eyes. Rapunzel is lost to you. You will never see her again!"

The king's son was beside himself with grief, and in his despair he jumped out of the tower window. He was not killed, but he fell into some thorn bushes, and the thorns blinded him.

He wandered blindly through the forest, eating nothing but roots
and berries, weeping and wailing for the loss of his beloved Rapunzel.

    So he wandered for several years, until at last he came to the deserted place where Rapunzel was living in great grief.

    All at once he heard a familiar voice. He went in the direction of that voice, and when he reached it, Rapunzel recognized him. She flung her arms around his neck and wept. Two of her tears fell on his eyes, and suddenly he could see as well as ever.

    He took Rapunzel home to his kingdom, where the people welcomed him back with joy, and Rapunzel and her prince lived happily ever after.

THE FROG PRINCE

Once, in olden times, when
wishes still had power, there
lived a king. All of his daughters
were beautiful, but the youngest
was the loveliest of all. Even the
sun itself, which sees so much,
was dazzled when its light shone
on her face.

Close to the king's castle was
a great dark forest. In that forest,
under an ancient lime tree, was
a well.

Often, on hot summer days, the king's youngest daughter would wander into the forest and sit down on the edge of the cool well. Then, to pass the time, she would play with a golden ball, throwing it into the air and catching it again. She loved this toy–it was her special treasure. But one day she failed to catch the ball when it fell. It hit the ground, then bounced straight into the water.

The princess gazed down into the depths, but the ball had disappeared. The well was so dark and deep that she could not tell what lay under the surface. She began to cry. Her sobs grew louder and louder, filling the air. She felt as if nothing could comfort her.

Suddenly she heard a voice. "Princess," it said, "whatever is the matter? Your howling would move the heart of a stone!"

Where did the voice come from? She looked around and saw a frog poking his big, ugly head out of the water. "So it was you speaking just now, old water-splasher!" she said scornfully. "Why am I crying? I'll tell you. My golden ball fell down the well, and now I've lost it forever."

"I can help you," said the frog. "But what will you give me if I bring back your plaything?"

"Whatever you want, dear frog," said the princess. "My finest clothes, my jewels, even my golden crown!"

"Oh, I don't want clothes and jewels, or other things of that kind," said the frog. "But I would like some love and affection. Now, if you promise to let me be your special friend and playmate, if you let me sit beside you at the dinner table, eat from your golden plate, drink from your golden cup, and sleep in your little bed–if you promise me these small things, I will dive down and bring back your golden ball."

"Yes, yes," said the princess. "I'll promise whatever you want if only you bring back my lovely ball!" But she thought to herself: The creature is talking nonsense. It's a frog! It lives in the water with other frogs. How can it come to court and behave as if it were human?

The frog, though, heard only the promise. He nodded, then dived down into the well. After a while he swam to the surface with the golden ball in his mouth, and shook it out onto the grass.

The princess was overjoyed to see her treasure again. She picked it up and rushed away. "Wait, wait!" cried the frog. "I can't run at that speed! Your legs are longer than mine!" But his croaking calls were wasted. The princess raced on, reached the castle, and put the frog out of her mind. The poor fellow turned away sadly, and went back into the well.

The next day the princess sat down in her usual place at the royal dinner table. She was about to take a cherry from her golden plate when she heard a peculiar noise—*splosh, splosh, flop, flop*—on the marble stairs. Something was crawling up, step-by-step. That something reached the door and stopped. It knocked: *tap, tap*. It spoke in a croaking voice. "King's daughter," it said, "open the door!"

Fearfully, the princess went to the door and peered outside. There was the frog, patiently waiting. She shut the door quickly and went back to her place at the table. Oh, she was afraid!

She sat quite still, but her heart beat fast—so fast that her father noticed. "Child," he said, "what is the matter? Is an ogre waiting outside to carry you off?"

"No, no," she said. "It isn't an ogre—it's a nasty frog."

"A frog? What does he want?" her father asked, surprised.

"Dear father, as I was playing by the well, my golden ball fell into the water. I was crying so hard that the frog offered to bring it back. Only he made me promise to let him be my playmate and sit next to me at the table. I never thought that he could leave the well and come to the palace. Now he is outside and wants to come in!"

At that moment the knocking started again–*Tap, tap! Tap, tap!*– and the listeners at the table heard these words:

There was a princess–
Open the door!
She made me a promise,
I'll tell you more!
A promise, a promise,
that she must keep.
I've come for food and
drink and sleep.
Princess, O princess,
you cannot hide!
Your frog companion
waits outside!

"Daughter," said the king. "If you made a promise, it must be kept. Go and open the door."

Slowly the princess did as she was told. At once the frog hopped in and followed her to her chair. Then he called out, "Lift me up!"

"Do as he says," the king commanded. But as soon as she had put the frog on the chair, he leapt onto the table.

"Move your golden plate nearer," he croaked, "and we can eat together."

The princess moved her plate, but it was easy to see that she was none too happy. The frog enjoyed the dinner–but what about the princess? Every morsel stuck in the poor girl's throat.

At last, the frog finished his meal and spoke again. "I have eaten all I want," he said. "Now I am tired. Kindly carry me to your room and put me in your silken bed, so we can go to sleep."

The king's daughter began to cry. She was really afraid of the frog, so cold to the touch—and now he wanted to sleep in her beautiful, clean bed!

But the king frowned, and said sternly, "If someone has helped you in a time of need, you must not scorn him when the need has gone."

What could she do? She picked up the frog between finger and thumb, carried him upstairs, and put him down in a corner.

She waited a little while, then went to bed.

But no sooner was her head on the pillow than she heard the frog creeping along the floor. "I am tired," he said. "I want to sleep comfortably, just as you do. Now pick me up, or I shall tell your father."

44

The princess was
enraged, but she
dared not refuse.
    She picked
up the frog and
then–with a rush
of anger–threw
him with all her
might against the
wall!
    As she did so,
she cried out:
"Now are you
satisfied, you
nasty creature?"

45

But as he fell, an
astonishing thing
happened. The frog
began to change his
shape. He was no longer
a frog, but a young and
handsome prince, gazing
at her with eyes that were
both beautiful and kind.

47

The prince had a strange tale to tell. A wicked witch had cast a spell on him, a spell that only the loveliest princess could break. And now he was free!

The king rejoiced at the news. He welcomed the prince as a husband for his daughter, and so the two were married.

"Tomorrow," the prince said to his bride, "we shall travel to my kingdom." Then they fell asleep.

In the morning, the sun woke them up. They saw that a carriage was waiting at the gates. It was drawn by eight white horses with white ostrich plumes on their heads and trappings all of gold.

At the back stood a servant with three iron bands around his chest. So great had been the man's grief when his master was bewitched, that he had placed the three bands around him to keep his heart from breaking.

"My faithful Henry!" said the prince, and greeted him joyfully.

And now the bride and bridegroom were ready to leave for the prince's own kingdom. Faithful Henry lifted each one into the carriage, then took his place behind them.

After they had driven a short distance, a sharp crack was heard. Startled, the bridegroom spoke: "Henry, Henry, what's that sound? Is the carriage breaking?"

Henry replied:

"No, Sire, 'tis a ring that bound
my heart when it was aching.
But now my lord is freed and back,
joy has made the iron crack!"

Then a second time they
heard a crack, and a third time
after that. Each time the prince
feared that the carriage was
breaking. But no—the sound
came from the last of the bands
freeing faithful Henry's heart.

Grief forged the bonds at first:
Grief for his lord accursed.
Joy made the bonds to burst.

55

THE SNOW QUEEN

Once upon a time, two poor children lived in an old city. They loved each other as if they were brother and sister. The boy was called Kay, and the girl's name was Gerda.

There were roses growing in the window boxes nearby, and the two children often sang a song that went like this:

In the vale grow roses wild,
Where we meet the Holy Child.

One winter day, when the windows were frozen over, the children were playing in the snow outside. "Ow!" cried Kay. "Something pricked my heart, and something flew into my eye!" But when Gerda looked, she couldn't see anything.

"I think it's gone now," said Kay, but it wasn't. Splinters of the Devil's mirror had just flown into his heart and eye.

"Why are you crying?" he asked Gerda roughly. "It makes you look so ugly!" And then he ran away.

As Kay ran down the street, a big white sleigh came driving along, drawn by white horses. Inside sat someone wrapped in white furs. Kay attached his own little sleigh and rode along behind it.

Soon both sleighs were speeding out of the city gates. Snow was falling fast, and Kay wanted to untie his sleigh, but couldn't. On went the sleighs, as fast as the wind, and the snowflakes grew larger and larger.

Then the white sleigh stopped, and the driver rose. She was covered with snow, and now Kay recognized her: she was the Snow Queen! She wrapped Kay in her fur coat, lifted him into her sleigh, and gave him an icy kiss on the forehead that went straight to his heart. For a moment Kay thought he was dying, but then he felt better. He forgot all about Gerda and his parents, and he no longer felt cold.

Soon they were flying through the air, while the cold wind blew and wolves howled below them.

When Kay did not come home that evening or the next, Gerda was in despair. She searched the whole city, but nobody had seen Kay. Gerda wept bitterly. It was a long, sad winter for her. But when spring came, Gerda put on her new red shoes and went to the river to look for Kay.

"Did you take my friend away?" she asked the river. "I will give you my new red shoes, my greatest treasure, if only you will give him back to me." She climbed into a boat that was lying by the bank, and threw her shoes into the water.

But the river did not reply. The boat drifted away on the current, faster and faster. Gerda was frightened and began to cry.

"Perhaps the river is taking me to Kay," she thought after a while, and stopped crying. The boat drifted toward the bank, where Gerda saw a thatched house standing in a cherry orchard. She called for help, and an old woman came out. Smiling, she drew the boat to the bank.

"Poor child, why are you drifting down this great river?" asked the old woman. Gerda told the woman her sad story. The old woman said that Kay had not yet passed by, but he might do so any day. She led Gerda inside and gave her delicious cherries to eat.

As Gerda ate, the old woman combed her hair with a golden comb, and gradually the little girl forgot her lost playmate.

The old woman was an enchantress, but not wicked. She wanted Gerda to stay with her because she was lonely, so she hurried out into the garden, touched the beautiful roses with her magic crook, and they all sank into the earth. She did not want them to remind Gerda of her home, where the roses grew in window boxes, for that would remind her of Kay, and then she would leave.

Then the old woman took Gerda into her flower garden. How beautiful and fragrant it was!

Gerda loved the garden. There were so many flowers, but one seemed to be missing, though she did not know which one.

One day, Gerda saw a rose on the enchantress's sun hat and remembered. She ran out into the garden. "Kay, Kay! I must find Kay!" she cried, and began to weep. As her tears fell on the ground, the roses grew again.

"Roses, do you know where Kay is? Is he dead?" Gerda asked them.

"We have been underground, but your Kay wasn't there," said the roses. "He is not dead."

How happy Gerda was! She ran out of the old enchantress's flower garden and into the wide world to look for Kay.

As Gerda left the garden, she left summer, too. In the forest, the leaves on the trees were already golden.

"Oh, I have wasted so much time!" sighed Gerda, and she ran until her feet were tired and sore and she had to rest. Suddenly a crow came hopping up to her.

"*Caw, caw!*" called the crow, flying on a little way ahead. Thinking the bird would lead her to Kay, Gerda followed it all the way to a castle. When the crow entered, so did she.

They went through many magnificent rooms until they reached a bedchamber with two golden beds in it. A Princess lay in one and a Prince lay in the other, but alas—no Kay! The Princess was very kind, and asked Gerda to tell her story.

"We will help you as much as we can," the Prince and Princess told her, and they gave her warm fur boots, a muff, and a golden coach for her travels. The Princess wished her luck, and Gerda went off.

She rode through a dark forest, where the golden coach shone like torchlight. Some robbers saw it, and hurried over.

"Gold!" they cried, "pure gold!" And they seized the horses' reins and took the coachman prisoner.

Suddenly a little robber girl appeared.

"I want to play with that girl!" she cried. "I want her muff and her boots, and I want her to sleep in my bed with me!"

The robbers drove on, farther into the forest.

"Are you a princess?" asked the little robber girl.

"No," said Gerda, and she told the little robber girl her story, and how much she loved Kay.

The coach stopped in the yard of the robbers' castle, which was half in ruins.

"You shall sleep with me tonight," said the little robber girl, laughing as she took a long knife out of a crack in the wall.

"What is that knife for?" asked Gerda, frightened.

"I always sleep with a knife beside me," said the little robber girl. "You never know what may happen."

But Gerda could not sleep. Then some doves began to coo.

"*Coo, coo, coo,* we have seen little Kay," said the doves. "He was in the Snow Queen's sleigh, riding away above the treetops. *Coo, coo.* Ask the reindeer. He knows the Snow Queen's realm!"

"Yes, my home is in the far north," sighed the reindeer. "But the Snow Queen's realm is even farther."

"Then Kay really is still alive," Gerda whispered. "Oh, Kay, I will go north and look for you!" Then she went to sleep at last, with new hope in her heart.

Early the next morning, Gerda told the robber girl what the doves had said, and the robber girl decided to give Gerda the reindeer and let her go.

"And here are your fur boots," said the little robber girl, "because it will be cold. But I'll keep the muff! It's too pretty for me to give back. However, I don't want you to freeze, so here are my mother's mittens to keep you warm, and food so you won't go hungry."

The robber girl undid the reindeer's chain and led him out of the castle. She put
Gerda on the animal's back, saying, "Off you go, and take good care!"

Gerda waved good-bye, and then the reindeer galloped away into the forest, as
fast as he could go.

The reindeer ran day and night. At last they came to Finland. The reindeer took
Gerda to an old Finnish woman who knew all the secrets of the far north. Her cottage
was so hot that Gerda had to take off her boots and mittens. The woman put a piece
of ice on the reindeer's head, and then the reindeer told her Gerda's story.

"I know how wise you are," said the reindeer. "Can't you give this little girl a potion that will make her strong enough to overcome the Snow Queen?"

The Finnish woman took the reindeer into a corner and whispered to him, "Kay is under the Snow Queen's spell, and has forgotten all about his parents and little Gerda."

"But couldn't you make her able to fight the Snow Queen's magic?" asked the reindeer.

"She is already very powerful," said the Finnish woman. "Her power lies in her loving heart! Even the wild robber girl granted her wishes. The Snow Queen's realm begins two miles from here. Take the little girl to the big bush with the red berries, and then hurry back!" After saying this, the Finnish woman put Gerda on the reindeer's back, and off he ran as fast as he could go.

"Oh, I forgot my boots and mittens!" cried Gerda, as the cold stabbed her like a knife. But the reindeer dared not turn back. On and on he ran.

When they reached the bush with the red berries, Gerda got down. The reindeer kissed her as he cried big, shiny tears. Then off he ran as fast as he could go, for he feared the Snow Queen's icy realm.

There stood poor Gerda, barefoot, in the middle of that terrible, ice-cold country.

In her despair, little Gerda prayed, and soon she was surrounded by angels who drove away the snow and the cold. Boldly Gerda went on, straight into the snowstorm.

The Snow Queen's magnificent palace was cold and gleaming and the halls lay empty in the northern light. Kay was all alone in one of them, playing with hard, shiny pieces of ice.

When Gerda saw him, she flung her arms around his neck. "Kay, dear Kay!" she cried, holding him tight. "I've found you at last!"

But Kay sat as if he were frozen. Seeing that, Gerda wept hot tears that fell on Kay's breast and flowed into his heart. They melted the lump of ice there, and dissolved the splinter of glass. Kay looked at Gerda, and she began to sing:

In the vale grow roses wild,
Where we meet the Holy Child.

Then Kay burst into tears, and soon the tiny piece of glass floated out of his eye. At last he recognized Gerda. "Gerda, dear little Gerda, where have you been so long?" he cried. They laughed and wept for joy.

Gerda kissed Kay's cheeks, eyes, hands, and feet until he felt warm again.

As they left the castle holding hands and talking about the roses at home, the icy winds died down and the sun came out.

When they came to the bush with the red berries, the reindeer was waiting with a sleigh and some warm clothes that the Finnish woman had given him. He accompanied the children to the border of that cold land.

"Good-bye!" called the reindeer. Suddenly, birds were singing, and the buds were green. Spring had come!

Gerda and Kay began their journey back. On their way, they met the little robber girl.

"I hope it was worth it, going to the ends of the earth for him!" she said to Gerda. "How did you find him?"

Gerda and Kay told their story, and the little robber girl smiled and promised to visit them one day. Then she rode away into the forest.

Next Gerda and Kay came to the castle where the Prince and Princess lived, and they were magnificently entertained there. Wherever they went, spring broke out.

Finally in the distance they heard church bells and saw the tall towers of their own city.

At home, everything was just as it used to be. But as they walked through the doorway, they realized they were grown-up now.

There were roses at the open window. Kay and Gerda held hands. They had forgotten all about the cold magnificence of the Snow Queen's realm, as if it were nothing but a bad dream.

Looking into each other's eyes, they understood the old song:

In the vale grow roses wild,
Where we meet the Holy Child.

There they stood happily, grown-up, yet still children at heart, and it was summer. Warm, glorious summer.

CINDERELLA

ONCE UPON A TIME there was a nobleman who married again after his first wife had died. His new bride was very haughty, and she had two daughters exactly like herself. The nobleman also had a daughter of his own, the best, sweetest girl in the world, just like her mother, who had been very kindhearted.

As soon as the wedding was over, the girl's stepmother showed her wicked nature. She could not bear to see how good and beautiful her stepdaughter was, for it made her own daughters seem even nastier.

The girl had to do all the unpleasant tasks about the house, scrubbing and sweeping and keeping her stepsisters' beautiful rooms clean and neat, while she herself slept on a wretched straw mattress in a little attic.

The poor girl bore it all meekly and didn't dare tell her father, who would not have believed her, for he was totally under his wife's control. When the girl's work was done, she would lie down by the ashes of the kitchen fire to get a little warmth. So everyone called her Cinderella.

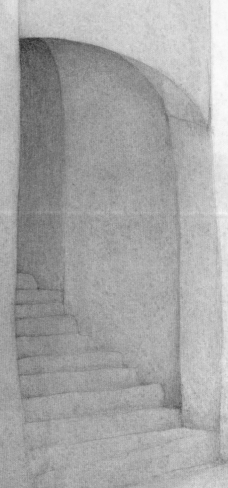

It happened one day that the king's son was to give a ball, and he invited all the nobility of the land, including Cinderella's two stepsisters.

Now there was even more work for Cinderella to do. She had to keep washing and ironing, bringing her stepsisters different dresses and shoes, then putting them away again, and brushing the sisters' hair in new ways. She did all she could to make them look beautiful, but even in her ragged clothes, she was a thousand times prettier than her stepsisters.

At last the great day came, and the sisters drove off to the ball. Sadly Cinderella watched them go, and she began to weep bitterly.

Now, Cinderella's godmother was a fairy, and she saw all this. "Do you want to go to the ball too?" she asked Cinderella.

"Oh, yes!" sighed Cinderella. "I would love to go!"

"Very well, then," said her godmother. "Go into the garden and fetch me a pumpkin."

Cinderella went into the garden, picked the best pumpkin she could find, and brought it back.

Her fairy godmother touched it with a magic wand and it turned into a coach made of pure gold.

Then the fairy turned six mice into a wonderful team of six beautiful white horses.

But they still needed a coachman, so the fairy touched a rat with her magic wand, and there stood a stout coachman wearing a very fine hat.

Next the fairy said, "Go into the garden and bring me the six lizards you will find behind the well!" And no sooner had Cinderella brought them than her fairy godmother turned them into six footmen.

"There!" Cinderella's fairy godmother told her. "Now you can go to the ball."

"Oh," said Cinderella, "but how can I go to the ball in these old rags?"

Then the fairy touched Cinderella herself with her magic wand, and there she stood in a dress of golden cloth covered with jewels. She wore glass slippers on her feet—the loveliest slippers ever seen.

Cinderella kissed her fairy godmother and climbed into the coach.

"Mind you don't stay after midnight," said the fairy, "or your coach will turn straight back into a pumpkin, your coachman into a rat, your horses into mice, your footmen into lizards, and your beautiful dress will be nothing but rags again."

Cinderella promised to do as her fairy godmother said, and she rode happily away.

When she came to the palace, the servants told the king's son that a noble princess had arrived, but no one knew who she was. He hurried to meet her, gave her his hand, and led her into the great ballroom.

The whole room suddenly fell silent. The dancing couples stood still; the violins stopped playing. Everyone gazed at Cinderella's radiant beauty, and then a whisper went around the ballroom. "Heavens above, how lovely she is!"

The king's son himself led Cinderella into the dance, and she danced so prettily that the guests admired her even more.

As for the prince, he had eyes for no one and nothing else. Even when the most delicious dishes were served for supper, he could not eat a morsel.

Then, suddenly, Cinderella heard the clock strike twelve. She curtsied quickly to the prince and hurried away. No one could stop her.

No sooner was Cinderella home than her dress turned back into rags again.

When her stepsisters got up at noon the next day, they found Cinderella cleaning the floor as usual. They told her how much they had enjoyed the ball, and all about the handsome prince, the wonderful music, and the beautiful unknown princess.

"Didn't anybody know her?" asked Cinderella.

"No, no one knew who she was. She disappeared at midnight, and she wasn't seen again."

Cinderella just smiled and went on washing the floor. Her stepsisters told her there was to be another ball that very evening, and they were both going.

So of course Cinderella went to the ball too. This time her fairy godmother gave her an even more beautiful dress, and rich jewels. The king's son did not move from her side all evening, and said a thousand kind and loving things to her, so that Cinderella quite forgot her promise to her fairy godmother.

When she heard the first stroke of midnight chime, however, she suddenly remembered. She tore herself away from the prince and ran off as fast as a deer.

At first the prince was rooted to the spot. Then he ran after Cinderella. He could not find her, but he did see one of her glass slippers, which she had lost as she ran. Tenderly he picked it up.

The palace guards were asked if they had seen a princess pass through the palace gates.

"No, we saw no one," they said. "At least, certainly not a princess. All we saw was a peasant girl dressed in rags."

Cinderella came home on foot and out of breath, without her coach or footmen. She had nothing left but one glass slipper.

Her two stepsisters told her how the beautiful unknown princess had disappeared again on the stroke of midnight. But she had lost a slipper, they added, and the prince had done nothing at all for the rest of the night but gaze at it. He seemed to have fallen head over heels in love with the mysterious princess.

A few days later the prince announced that he meant to marry the girl whose foot would fit the glass slipper. First all the princesses in the country tried it on, and then the countesses, and then all the other ladies of the court, but it was too small for any of them.

At last the slipper was brought to Cinderella's house, and her stepsisters tried it on, but it did not fit them, either.

"May I try?" asked Cinderella.

At that her sisters laughed mockingly, but the nobleman who was taking the slipper around the town looked closely at Cinderella and thought she was very beautiful.

"By all means," he said with a smile.

The sisters stared in amazement when they saw that the slipper fit Cinderella perfectly.

They were even more astonished when Cinderella took the other slipper out of her pocket and put it on, and when her fairy godmother arrived at that very moment and turned her rags into the most beautiful dress ever seen, they recognized her as the unknown princess.

They begged Cinderella to forgive them for all the harm they had done her, and she forgave them with all her heart.

Then Cinderella was taken to the prince, and a few days later they were married.

THE PRINCESS AND THE PEA

There was once a prince who wished to marry a princess, but she had to be a real princess.

He traveled the whole world over hoping to find such a young lady and discovered that there were plenty of princesses, but whether they were real or not, he just couldn't tell. There was something about all of them that was not quite right. So he returned home feeling miserable because he wanted so much to marry a princess.

105

One evening there was a terrible storm; thunder rolled, lightning flashed, and rain was pouring down. Then there was a loud knock at the door, and the king went down to open it.

A princess was standing outside, but goodness, what a state she was in! Rain was streaming from her hair, dripping from her clothes, and sloshing out of her shoes, but she claimed that she was a real princess.

We'll soon see about that! thought the queen. And she said to the servants, "Go to the garden and fetch me a pea."

She took the pea, went into a bedroom, lifted all the bedclothes off the bed and put the pea under them.

The she took twenty mattresses, laid them on top of the pea and then took twenty quilts and put them on top of the mattresses.

This was where the Princess was to sleep
that night.

The next morning the king and queen asked the princess how she had slept.

"Terribly," said the princess. "I scarcely closed my eyes all night. Goodness knows what was in my bed, but it was something hard and it's made me black and blue all over. It was dreadful!"

Now they could tell that she must be a real princess, because she had felt the tiny pea through twenty mattresses and twenty quilts. No one but a princess could be so sensitive.

So the prince asked her to be his bride, for at last he had found a real princess.

122

123

The pea was put in a glass case and
is still there, unless someone has carried
it off. So you see, this is a true story!

And they all lived happily ever after.